ZACK, ZOE & JAMES -

MAY you ALWAYS FOLLOW
THE EXAMPLES of YOUR
GRANDPARENTS TO ALWAYS
LOOK FOR THE BEST IN
PEOPLE! GOD BLESS

5/21

HEART of a HERO
The story of Pixie the three-legged dog

Written by **Kenny Parcell** • Pictures by **Julie Olson**

To all those who see the inner spirit rather than the outward appearance.
-K.P.

To my supporters who cheer me on. You are heroes to me.
-J.O.

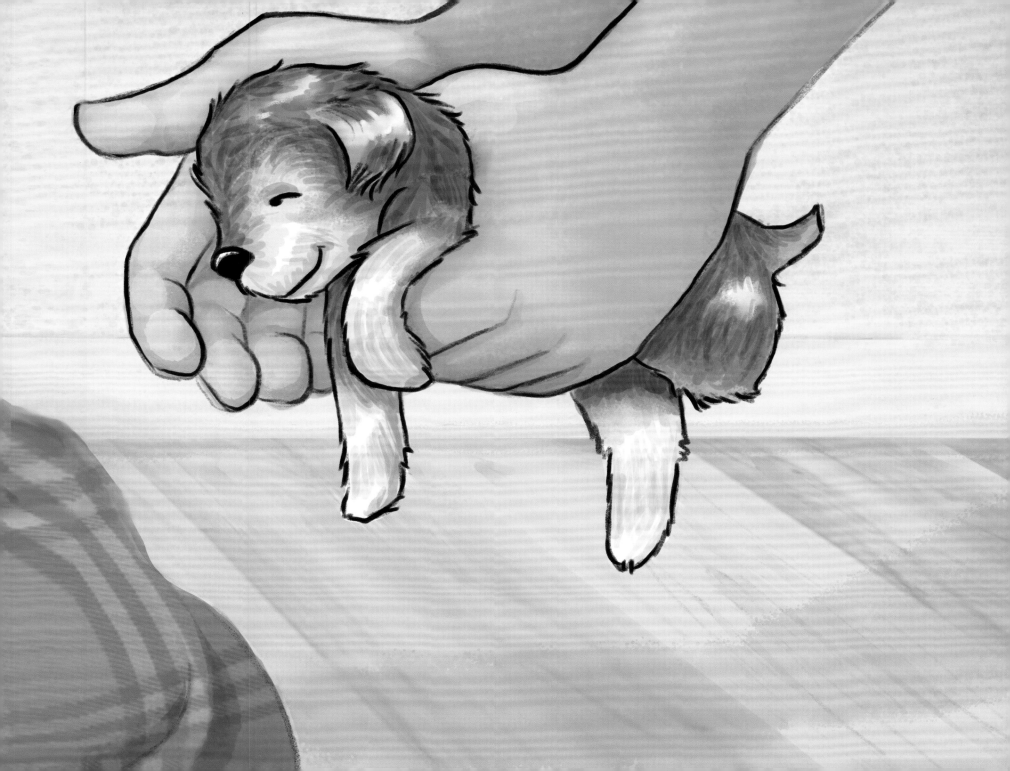

Today was the day!

For an entire year, eight-year-old Sammy worked hard in school and did all her chores without complaining, with the hope of getting a puppy. Now it was her parents' turn to keep their end of the bargain.

Sammy wondered how she'd know which puppy to pick.
Her dad said there were five or six for sale.
"What if each one is as cute as the other?"
asked Sammy. Her mom gave her some
advice.

The owner of the puppies welcomed Sammy and her parents inside.
"You're the first one to arrive, so you can have the pick of the litter.
Choose any puppy you'd like."

Sammy picked up five furry bundles, one at a time. She'd scratch behind its ear,
look into its eyes, and then set it down. But the sixth puppy, she didn't put down.
As she stared into its eyes, she knew this was the one. The puppy's three
little legs wiggled with excitement.

The owner said, "You don't want that one. It's missing a leg."
"I know," Sammy replied. "But she's the one." She turned to the owner
and asked, "How much for this one?"
The owner shook her head and said, "The other puppies
are two hundred dollars each, but that one is free to a good home."

Sammy stood up, clutching the puppy tight. "Well, just because she is missing a leg, doesn't mean she's any less of a dog at heart."

Before her parents could say a word, Sammy reached into her pocket and pulled out two hundred dollars. She handed the money to the owner and marched to the car with her very own three-legged dog.

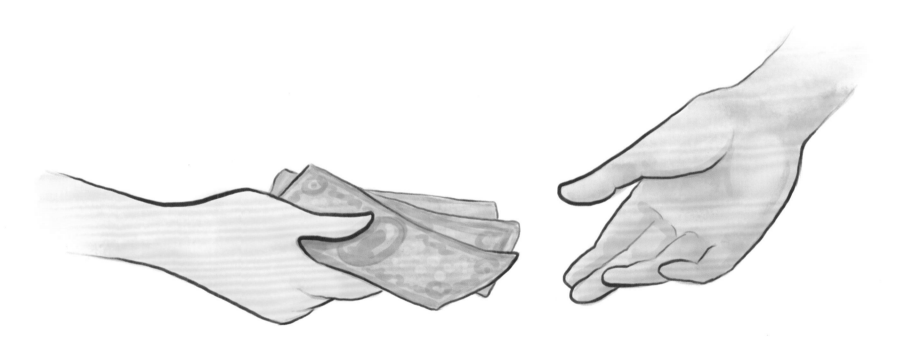

"I love that name," said Mckell. "Can we hold her?"
Kelsey tickled the puppy's belly and gasped. "Sammy! Pixie only has three legs.
Weren't there any other dogs with four?"

"Of course," said Sammy. "But she had the
most personality and
the most heart."

Before long, the whole neighborhood was cheering for the little three-legged dog.

"Yay, Pixie!" they called out.

Pixie could shake hands, play dead,

and roll over.

Pixie could even jump and catch her treat in mid-air. But Pixie wasn't only good at tricks.

One day, Sammy and her friends were playing when their ball bounced out into the street. Sammy started to run after it. All of a sudden, Pixie jumped in front of her.

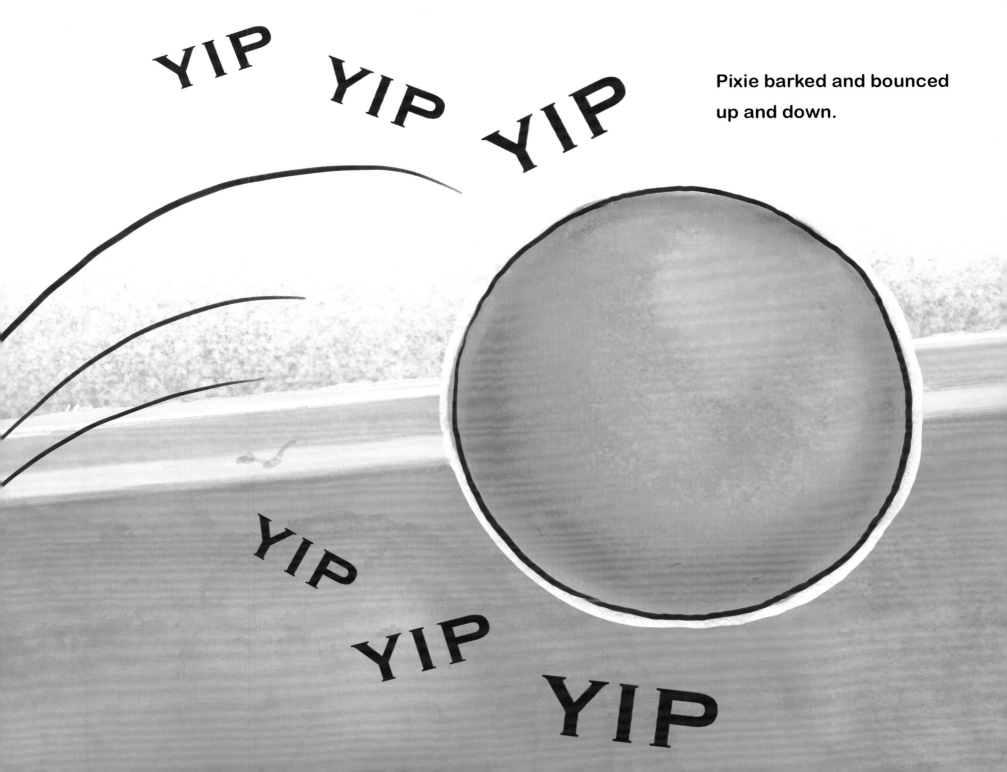

YIP YIP YIP

YIP

YIP

YIP

Pixie barked and bounced up and down.

Sammy hadn't seen it coming, but a car screeched to a stop just a few feet away. There was a loud POP as it hit her ball.

The driver jumped out and exclaimed, "That dog just saved your life!"

Sammy's parents and the neighbors heard the commotion and came running.

"Is everyone okay?" they asked again and again.

Pixie bounded over to Sammy, Kelsey and Mckell. She licked, yapped, and bounced around some more.

"Yes," Sammy said. "Thanks to Pixie, we're all okay."

Pretty soon,
everyone in town knew what the
little three-legged dog had done.

And when asked how Pixie had done it, Sammy said,

It's not what's on the outside that counts, it's what's on the inside, and...

Three Legged Dog has the Heart of a Hero

One might expect some act of heroics on the part of a parent or a close friend or even emergency workers. But who would expect that a tiny dog with only three legs would be the reason 3 little girls are alive today. On Wednesday, August 21, Pixie, the three legged dog barked her little heart out to prevent Sammy, Kelsey and Mckell from entering the street where their ball had bounced.

Sammy, Kelsey and Mckell had not noticed the car that was coming down the street at that moment, but their tiny dog did. Pixie jumped and yapped in warning and the girls stopped at the curb just as the oncoming car hit and popped the ball that had bounced in front of it. Had Pixie not stopped the girls, they may have tragically been hit instead.

Sammy chose Pixie from a litter of 6 puppies and decided that even though the puppy was missing a leg, she had something special inside. The owner of the puppies was ready to ... the puppy for ... of the lack

was being asked for the puppies with four legs. Some may say, that act makes Sammy a hero as well. No matter how you look at it...a girl who saves a dog or a dog who saves a girl, more than one hero exists in this story. Hopefully, we ...ll develop similar

You Can Be a Hero
MAKE A DIFFERENCE TODAY

Here is a list of places you can go to volunteer or ideas to implement that may make a difference around where you live. But really the idea is simple. Just look out for others and treat them as the ...luence

Author's Note

I always wondered why some people with so much achieved so little and some with so little could achieve so much. So many people today make judgments about someone's outward appearance or dress without really getting to know what's inside someone's heart. This book was conceived of and created to encourage others to strive to be more like the character Sammy. I would love for everyone to realize that outward appearance means very little, and it is what is on inside that really counts. Everyone has a heart of a hero. Sometimes they just need to search harder to find it, because other people also need them to find it.

- Kenny Parcell

text copyright © 2020 Kenny Parcell
illustrations copyright © 2020 Julie Olson

Edited and Designed by Julie Olson
printed and bound in China

Published by:

Kenny Parcell
648 N 900 E #9
Spanish Fork, UT 84660

Library of Congress Cataloging-in-Publication Data
Parcell, Kenny
Heart of a Hero The story of Pixie the three legged dog / by Kenny Parcell, Illustrated by Julie Olson. 1st ed.

ISBN: 978-0-578-74594-7
Work is categorized as Book, Poetry, Written Work
Copyright Year: 2020